Birthday Bling

To my wonderful neighbors, Gemma
and the real Julian J.
—C.D.

To Claire, Christian and Marie-Pierre
—G.K.

Copyright © 2024 by Astra Publishing House
All rights reserved. Copying or digitizing this book for storage, display,
or distribution in any other medium is strictly prohibited.
For information about permission, contact the publisher through
its website: astrapublishinghouse.com

Kane Press
An imprint of Astra Books for Young Readers,
a division of Astra Publishing House
kanepress.com
Printed in the United States

Library of Congress Cataloging-in-Publication Data

Names: Daly, Catherine R., author. | Kote, Genevieve, illustrator.
Title: Birthday bling / by Catherine R. Daly ;
illustrated by Genevieve Kote.
Description: First edition. | New York : Kane Press, an imprint of ASTRA
Books for young readers, 2024. | "Dollars to doughnuts"—Title page. |
Summary: "An early chapter book designed to help kids decipher finance
facts and fallacies. Lucy and her best friend, Julian, find out about
the pros and cons of gift cards versus credit cards"—Provided by publisher.
Identifiers: LCCN 2023026935 (print) | LCCN 2023026936 (ebook) |
ISBN 9781662670527 (hardcover) | ISBN 9781662670213 (trade paperback) |
ISBN 9781662670220 (ebk)
Subjects: LCSH: Children—Finance, Personal—Juvenile literature. |
Finance, Personal—Juvenile literature.
Classification: LCC HG179 .D32575 2024 (print) | LCC HG179 (ebook) | DDC
332.0240083—dc23/eng/20230905
LC record available at https://lccn.loc.gov/2023026935
LC ebook record available at https://lccn.loc.gov/2023026936

2 4 6 8 10 9 7 5 3 1

Spending & Credit

Birthday Bling

by Catherine R. Daly
illustrated by Genevieve Kote

KANEPRESS
AN IMPRINT OF ASTRA BOOKS FOR YOUNG READERS
New York

CHAPTER ONE

"I spy with my little eye, something that begins with *P*," Lucy said.

Julian scanned the busy street. "Pizza parlor? Police officer? Pothole?"

"Nope, nope, nope," replied Lucy.

"Money!" cried Julian.

Lucy shook her head. "No, silly. Pigeon! Money doesn't start with *P*!" She gave her best friend an annoyed look. They liked to play games on their morning walk to school. But it usually went a little better than this.

"I mean I found money," said Julian. He bent down and picked a bill off the sidewalk.

"Oh!" Lucy came to a stop beside him. "How much?"

Julian held up a crisp ten-dollar bill. He immediately turned to an elderly man standing nearby.

"Excuse me," he said. "Is this yours?"

The man gazed at Julian through his thick eyeglasses. "Let's see, is it green and rectangular?" he asked.

"Um . . . yeah," said Julian.

The old man laughed. "Just kidding, son. The owner of that bill is probably long gone. It belongs to you now!"

Lucy and Julian grinned at each other.

"We should use it to get ice cream after school," said Lucy. At the very same time Julian said, "We should save it."

Lucy rolled her eyes. "I guess it's up to you since you found it. But we haven't been to What's the Scoop in ages."

Julian folded the bill neatly and put it into his backpack. "I *will* save it," he said. "I feel like we might be having some ice cream this weekend, anyway."

"This weekend?" Lucy said. Then she laughed. "Oh, you mean at my birthday party? Yeah, something like that."

Lucy was having a rock-climbing birthday party on Saturday, just five days away. She was going to turn ten—double digits! Julian's birthday wasn't until

September. He'd be just one digit for many more months to come. He didn't mind. Much anyway.

They resumed walking. "I spy with my little eye, something that begins with . . ." Julian looked up and down the block. "*A*," he finished.

Lucy scanned the area. "Um, apartment building? Air conditioner?" She looked up. "Airplane?"

"Nope," said Julian mysteriously.

Just then Lucy recognized the person walking ahead of them. She stopped short.

"Avery?" she whispered. "Not funny, Julian! Let's walk slowly so we don't catch up with her."

Avery was a new girl at their school.

She had the coolest sneakers and the fanciest backpack in the entire class, but everyone said that she was stuck-up and spoiled rotten. Plus, she talked like a grown-up sometimes. It was kind of annoying.

"I heard she lives in a huge apartment and has a whole wing to herself," said Lucy.

"Oh wow." Julian's eyes got wide. "Um, what's a wing?"

"I'm not exactly sure," said Lucy, "but it sounds fancy!"

They lagged behind, hoping that she wouldn't notice them. When Avery stopped at the next corner for the light to change, they waited several feet short of the curb. It seemed like they were in the clear, but then Avery turned and spotted them. "Hey, Lucy and Julian!" she cried, waving.

Lucy gave a quiet sigh. "Hi, Avery," she said. She and Julian stepped up next to her.

"How was your weekend?" Avery asked. "Let me guess. You watched a scary movie together!"

Julian cut his eyes toward Lucy. Huh, Avery had remembered that they rented a different horror movie every weekend?

"You know it," he said easily. "We baked monster cookies and watched *Frankenstein* with Boris Karloff."

Avery nodded. "A horror classic," she said. "Well, I went shopping and look at what I got!"

She opened her jeans jacket to reveal a sparkly sweatshirt. A very sparkly sweatshirt. Julian had to shield his eyes as the sunlight flashed off it. Meanwhile Lucy just stared at the sweatshirt, her mouth wide.

Julian almost laughed at Lucy. Then he did a double take. Wait a second, did she actually *like* it?

"Where did you get it?" Lucy asked.

"At this trendy little store called Zelda's," replied Avery. "I used my credit card!" She pulled a plastic card from the front pocket of her jacket.

Lucy gave Julian a knowing look. It said: *Told you, spoiled!*

Julian smirked. Thankfully his best friend was acting like herself again. "You have a credit card?" he asked. He thought they were only for grown-ups.

"Yeah," Avery said. "I use it for snacks and shopping and other necessities. My parents got tired of giving me cash all the time."

Julian grunted as Lucy elbowed him

in the ribs. Avery didn't notice. She was listing all the places she liked to go for after-school treats. Shortly after that, they arrived at school and joined the students heading inside. They lost sight of Avery.

"You didn't really like that sweatshirt, did you?" Julian asked as they climbed the stairs. The sweatshirt was the opposite of Lucy. She always wore baseball caps, jerseys, and sweatpants with the logos of her favorite teams on them. Not sparkles!

Lucy shrugged. "It was really pretty," she said. "And very shiny."

Julian thought about that for a minute, then suggested, "You should ask your mom to get it for you for your birthday."

"Yeah, maybe," Lucy muttered. She looked away.

Julian suddenly stopped short in the middle of the hallway. "Wait, are you afraid she will make a big deal out of you asking for something kind of girlie?"

"Yeah, maybe," Lucy repeated. She sighed. Her mom was always trying to make her wear dresses and skirts. If Lucy asked for something sparkly for her birthday, she was sure her mom would get so excited it would be totally embarrassing.

When they got to their classroom, backpacks had to be emptied, lunches put in the lunch bin, and homework turned in. Then class began. By lunchtime, when the two friends had a chance to talk again, the shiny sweatshirt was forgotten.

At least by Julian, that is.

CHAPTER TWO

Lucy squeezed Julian's hand in the elevator on Saturday morning. "I can't believe I'm ten today!" she said. "I'm so excited for my party!"

Julian managed a smile. "Yeah, me, too," he said.

"Liar," she said. "But I like your positive attitude."

When they reached the lobby of their building, Henry, the day doorman, greeted them with a big grin. "Well, if it isn't my two favorite pals, Lucian and Juicy!"

They laughed. Henry was their favorite, too.

"Hey, Henry," said Lucy. "Can you call me a cab?"

"You're a cab!" said Henry.

They waved goodbye as they walked outside. Lucy's mom was waiting at the curb in their minivan.

Julian stared out the window on the drive to Rock Your World. His stomach was doing little flips.

"Don't worry," Lucy said. "This can't be any worse for you than my skateboarding party."

Julian shrugged. That year he had found

out that he was really, really untalented at skateboarding. The paintball party was even worse. Those pellets hurt!

Honestly, Lucy's parties stressed him out. But he always tried to be a good sport.

When they got to Rock Your World, he helped Lucy and her mom decorate the party room. They blew up balloons and hung streamers. The other guests arrived, mostly kids from Lucy's soccer team. He was friendly to them all, even though he was a little in awe of their sportiness.

Then it was time to climb. Staring up at the massive wall, he broke out into a sweat. But still, he stepped right into the harness, like everybody else. And even though it gave him a killer wedgie, he took

a deep breath and inched his way up the wall. He carefully placed his fingers and toes on the handholds and footholds. He made sure to not look down. It was very slow going. He had made it only halfway up when the whistle blew. Their time was over. He breathed a sigh of relief as he was lowered to the ground. *Safe for another year!* he thought. Lucy, of course, had made it to the top. More than once.

Lucy's mom brought out pizza. And then a cake made entirely of doughnuts— Lucy's favorite treat. They were piled high on a platter and covered with whipped cream and strawberries.

"This is the best birthday ever!" Lucy said, biting into a blackberry jelly doughnut. A little jam dotted her chin, but she didn't seem to care. She couldn't wait to start opening gifts!

Lucy tore open the brightly colored paper to find a personalized water bottle, a stadium seat cushion from her favorite minor league baseball team, the Davis Dragons, and various jerseys and caps. Was Julian mistaken or did she look a little bit disappointed?

"Another jersey," she said. "Thanks!"

She did break into a big smile at his gift, a framed movie still from *The Wolf Man*. And then she opened an envelope from her Aunt Becky.

"Ooooh!" Lucy held up a plastic card. It

looked a lot like the one Avery had shown them.

"Happy birthday, Lucy!" said Aunt Becky. "I thought you might have fun picking out your own birthday gift."

Lucy grinned. "I sure will!" she said.

CHAPTER THREE

"I hate to brag, but I'm pretty sure my noodles were the best," Lucy bragged.

"True, but mine were pretty buttery," Julian put in.

Lucy nodded. "Totally."

The two friends were walking home late Thursday afternoon. Every week they went to cooking club together. They were convinced that Ms. Clark, the teacher who ran it, did not know how to cook. She wouldn't let them use anything that plugged in and always picked a recipe that didn't need sharp tools. Today they made buttered noodles for goodness' sake! Cooking club was pretty boring.

Suddenly, Lucy took an unexpected turn onto Beech Street.

"Where are we going?" Julian jogged to catch up.

"You'll see," Lucy said mysteriously. Another turn and then Lucy stopped in front of a store. Mannequins wearing trendy outfits posed in the window. The front doors stood wide open. Loud music spilled out.

Julian saw some older girls inside. They might even be in high school. He glanced at Lucy.

"What is this place?" he asked.

"You'll see," Lucy said again. She bit her lip nervously, but it was clear she wanted to go in.

"Come on." Julian stepped through the doors. "I could use a new . . ." He looked around the store. "Tube top?" he said.

Lucy laughed. "Definitely," she said.

Julian and Lucy wandered around. They passed crop tops, ruffled skirts, and neon shorts. Julian frowned. Lucy didn't wear any of this stuff. What were they doing here? But Lucy looked very focused, so he didn't ask out loud. Finally, she stopped in front of a display of sweatshirts. The very same sparkly one that Avery had been wearing the other day.

Now Julian got it. Lucy grabbed one off the rack. She checked the size and

looked uncertain for a moment. Julian stole a glance at the price tag and gulped. Expensive!

"Do you want to try that on?"

They spun around. A teenage girl wearing ripped jeans stood there.

"No!" said Lucy. "I mean, no thank you." She took a deep breath. "I'll just pay for this now." She headed to the cashier. Julian followed right behind her.

"Did you find everything you wanted?" asked the boy behind the counter. He had a nose ring and green hair. Julian thought he looked really cool.

When Lucy nodded, he rang up the sweatshirt. Lucy handed him her card. He scanned it. "And how will you pay for the rest?" he asked her.

Lucy just stared. "The rest of what?"

"The rest of the balance," he said. "What you owe."

"What do you mean?" Lucy asked. "I gave you my card."

"Right," he said. "But it only covers half the cost."

"But . . . but . . . I don't get it. I gave you my card," Lucy repeated.

The cashier tried again. "Do you have another card? Or cash?"

Lucy shook her head. "No."

"I'm sorry," said the cashier. "I'll have to return your card to you."

Lucy stared at her high tops. The cashier punched some info into his computer. He scanned the card again and handed it back to her. Without a word, she hurried out of the store. Julian followed behind.

"Why didn't my credit card work?" Lucy asked once they were back on the sidewalk.

"I have no idea," said Julian. "That was really weird."

Lucy sighed. "Now I'll never get that beautiful sweatshirt."

Beautiful? Julian shot her a funny look. But she seemed so disappointed that on the way home he gave her his entire last stick of gum, instead of splitting it, as he had kind of wanted to.

CHAPTER FOUR

"Hey!" said Julian as they stepped into the elevator. "I just remembered something! My parents are going out for dinner with your mom tonight. Oona is babysitting."

Lucy brightened. "That's right," she said. "I know! I'll ask Oona about the credit card."

Oona lived in their building. She was an actual sophomore in high school. She was smart and funny and she never got mad, like other babysitters sometimes did. If they spilled something she'd say, "Hey, it happens. Let's clean it up together." If they wanted to play a fifth game of Mouse Trap, which took a million years to set up, she'd say, "Awesome! You read my mind!"

Lucy pushed the button for Julian's floor and led the way to his apartment. It was practically her second home after all. Their moms had met in the elevator when they were pregnant and hit it off. And ever since Julian and Lucy started preschool together, they had been best friends.

The doorbell rang minutes after Julian and Lucy entered the apartment. Julian's twin four-year-old sisters, Abigail and Gabriella, ran to the door to greet Oona.

"If it isn't Abby and Gabby!" Oona said.

"What did you bring us?" they cried, jumping up and down.

"Girls! Really!" said Julian's mom. She stood in the living room, fastening her bracelet.

Oona laughed. "It's okay." She pulled out colorful construction paper, a big jar of glitter, glue, and some chopsticks from her tote bag. "Guess what? We're going to make crowns and magic wands tonight!"

"Yay!" the twins cheered. They were in a serious fairy princess phase.

"And I didn't forget you two," Oona said to Julian and Lucy, presenting them with a bag of Grim Reaper Tortilla Chips.

"Fire and Brimstone flavor!" Julian said happily. "Where did you get them? They're impossible to find!"

"I have my ways," Oona said mysteriously.

Oona, Abby, and Gabby made fairy

princess crowns and magic wands. After dinner and a parade around the apartment, Oona put the little girls to bed.

Finally, Lucy and Julian had her to themselves!

"So what are you working on these days?" Oona asked Julian.

Lucy fidgeted as Julian pulled out his sketchbook and showed Oona his latest character. Comics were his passion, especially superheroes.

"I love the bright green costume," Oona said. "What's the character's name?"

Julian sighed. "I haven't figured it out yet."

Oona smiled. "You will."

Lucy jumped in before Julian and Oona could get too deep into comic talk. "I have something really important to ask you," Lucy said. "For my birthday, I got a lot of great gifts. Including a credit card from my Aunt Becky!"

"Wow," said Oona, raising her eyebrows. "And happy birthday!"

"Then I tried to buy a sweatshirt at this store called Zelda's."

"A sparkly sweatshirt," added Julian.

Oona nodded. "That store is pretty expensive," she said.

"The cashier told me I didn't have enough money," Lucy said. "It didn't make any sense."

"It was really weird," Julian added. "Do you think maybe he made a mistake?"

"Do you have the card?" Oona asked.

Lucy fished it out of her pocket.

Oona held it up. "Aha," she said. "I see the problem. This isn't a credit card."

Lucy stared. "Then what is it?"

"It's a gift card," Oona told her.

Lucy felt her face get red. "A *what*?"

CHAPTER FIVE

"A gift card," Oona repeated.

"What's the difference?" Julian asked.

"A gift card has a specific amount of money on it. The sweatshirt that you wanted probably cost more money than the card is worth."

"Ohhhhh," said Lucy. "But it *looks* just like a credit card."

"It does," Oona agreed sympathetically. "But it's very different. Say your aunt put twenty-five dollars on it. Then that's all you have. No more. A credit card, on the other hand, can be used to buy a lot more. Sometimes thousands of dollars more."

"That sounds way better than a gift card!" said Lucy.

"But a gift card is like cash. When you use a credit card, you're *borrowing* the money. And that means you'll have to pay it back," explained Oona.

"What happens if you don't pay it back right away?" asked Lucy.

Set amount
May be limited to one store
No surprise fees
Can be used like cash

No set amount
Use to shop anywhere
Buy now, pay later

"If you don't pay anything at all, you get charged a late fee," Oona told her. "If you don't pay it back in full, you get charged interest."

"Interest?" Lucy echoed.

"Interest is a percentage of the money that you owe. So, you see, the item that you bought could end up costing you a lot more than the original price."

"I don't understand," said Lucy. She turned to Julian. "Do you?"

Julian shook his head. This credit card stuff was very confusing.

Oona bit her lip. She was thinking. Then she looked over to the corner of the living room where the twins' toys were stored. "I've got it!" she said.

She grabbed the Monopoly box from

a nearby shelf and took out a hundred dollars. She gave $50 to Julian and $50 to Lucy.

"Let's say Julian wants to buy some groceries." She pointed across the room to the twins' play kitchen. "Why don't you go shopping, Julian?" she told him.

Julian shrugged. "Okay," he said as he walked across the living room. He picked up the twins' mini shopping basket and filled it with play food—an apple, a can of alphabet soup, a carton of milk, a bunch of carrots, and a box of cereal.

"Are you ready to check out?" Oona said. She pretended to scan the groceries. "That will be twenty dollars please."

Julian handed her a bill.

"Thank you." Oona turned to Lucy.

"Now it's your turn," she said. Lucy grabbed the basket and stuffed it with a tub of ice cream, a box of crackers, a banana, an orange, and an artichoke.

"Did you find everything you were looking for?" Oona asked.

Lucy shrugged. "Not really. I don't like artichokes. But Julian took the carrots."

Oona laughed. Again, she pretend scanned the groceries. "That will be twenty dollars," she said.

Lucy reached for her money.

"This time, use your credit card," Oona told her.

Lucy pretended to hand over a credit card, and Oona pretended to scan it.

"Thank you. Have a nice day," said Oona.

Lucy pointed to her cash. "Look," she said. "Now Julian only has thirty dollars left. I still have fifty."

Oona held up a hand. "But wait. Later that month you also buy yourself a sparkly sweatshirt with your credit card. And when your credit card bill comes, you will owe seventy dollars."

"Oh," said Lucy. She held up her cash. "But I don't have seventy dollars. I only have fifty."

"Thank you very much," said Oona, taking the money from her. "You still owe the credit card company twenty dollars. And that's where the interest comes in. It's usually around fifteen to twenty percent of what you owe. So your groceries will end up costing *more* than twenty dollars. Even

if you pay it in full the following month, your twenty dollars of groceries could cost you twenty-four dollars. And if you take months to pay it off, it can really add up."

Lucy's eyes flew open. "That's terrible!" she said. "Credit cards sound bad!"

"Yeah! Why do so many people have them?" asked Julian.

Oona smiled. "Well, you can use them wisely," she said. "By spending what you can afford. You have to pay off your credit card in full each month."

"Why not just pay for the things you buy in cash?" Julian asked.

Oona pointed to the television. "Say you need to buy something expensive, like a new TV. It would be hard to carry around enough cash to pay for it, right?"

Lucy considered that. "There's this girl from school named Avery who has a card. Do you think it's a gift card or a credit card?" she wondered.

"I'd bet dollars to doughnuts that it's a debit card," said Oona.

Lucy's eyes lit up. "Dollars to doughnuts!" she said. "That's funny, Oona. What does it mean?"

"It's like saying I feel confident that what I said is true," said Oona. "With a debit card the money comes right out of your bank account. It keeps you from spending more money than you have. I'd guess Avery has a prepaid debit card. Her parents probably put a set amount onto the card every month. It will stop working when she reaches her monthly limit."

Lucy sighed. "So Avery's credit card is really a debit card. My credit card is really a gift card. And there's not enough on it to buy my sparkly sweatshirt." She looked sad.

"You can have the ten dollars I found on the street," Julian offered.

Lucy smiled gratefully at her friend. "You keep it," she told him. "I need a lot more money for the sweatshirt anyway."

CHAPTER SIX

"I spy with my little eye something that begins with—"

Lucy cut Julian off. "Sorry, I don't really feel like playing this morning."

"Sure," Julian said. It was clear his friend was still feeling bad about the sweatshirt.

Lucy reached up and ran her hand through her hair. Julian blinked as something flashed in the morning sun.

Julian peered closely. "Did you wear that shirt yesterday?" he asked. "When

Abby and Gabby made the fairy crowns?"

"Are you outfit shaming me?" Lucy cried. She looked a little embarrassed.

"No shame," said Julian. "It's just that I think you got glue and glitter all over your sleeve last night."

"Oh no!" said Lucy. "Is it noticeable?"

Julian burst out laughing.

"This isn't funny, Julian!"

"It isn't," Julian agreed. "But it's giving me an idea about that sweatshirt you want so much."

"Tell me!" Lucy demanded.

But Julian shook his head. "Patience, my friend," he said.

All day, Lucy kept trying to get Julian to spill the beans. All day, Julian kept saying no. Even as the last bell rang, Julian stayed quiet while they packed their backpacks, walked down the stairs, and out the doors. At last, he broke the silence.

"Follow me," he said. "We're going shopping."

"Wh—" Lucy started to say, but Julian had already taken off. She had to run to catch up.

Lucy followed Julian down the street. He then made a left on 15th Street, and finally came to a stop in front of a large store.

Lucy looked up. "Hearts and Crafts?" she said.

Without a word, Julian headed inside. Lucy trailed him up and down the aisles until he found what he was looking for.

"The Blinginator?" said Lucy.

"The Blinginator," Julian confirmed. "I saw it on TV last week! It's a machine you use to put rhinestones on any and everything—sweatshirts, jeans, socks,

backpacks." He held up the box. "You can make your own sparkly sweatshirt!"

Lucy shook her head. "It's not the same."

"It's better!" said Julian. "Because you'll make it just the way you like it. It would be one of a kind. Plus, you'll save so much money!"

"But I'll have to buy the Blinginator *and* a sweatshirt to decorate. How is that saving money?" Lucy asked.

"For the price of the sweatshirt from Zelda's you could buy the Blinginator, a pack of three plain sweatshirts, and take your best friend out for ice cream," he said. "Twice."

Lucy still did not look convinced, not one bit.

"And you'll always have the Blinginator," said Julian. "You could make yourself sparkly sweatshirts all the time. It will practically pay for itself!"

"I get it," Lucy said. A smile crept over her face as she reached into her pocket and pulled out her gift card. "But there's just one thing. I don't want a blingy sweatshirt anymore."

"Huh?" said Julian.

CHAPTER SEVEN

"Where's your partner in crime?" Henry asked the next morning when Julian stepped out of the elevator alone.

"She skipped breakfast," Julian told him. "She's meeting me in the lobby."

"What did she miss out on?" Henry asked. He knew that Julian's mom always made special breakfasts for both of them. She was a chef, after all.

"Blueberry pancakes," said Julian.

"Bummer," said Henry.

The elevator door opened with a loud *ding* and Lucy stepped out.

"Holy guacamole!" said Henry. "That is one glittery garment!"

Lucy smiled proudly. She turned to Julian. "I told you I didn't want a sparkly sweatshirt anymore. I wanted to make something that was more my style!"

"Wow," said Julian. "Just wow."

$ $ $

"Hey, wait up!" Julian and Lucy had just left school. They spun around to find Avery running to catch up with them.

"I've been staring at your jersey all day!" Avery said. "It's truly a work of art. Sean Decker from the Davis Dragons, amirite? All blinged out! I love it!"

Lucy looked at Avery with new respect. "You're right!"

"Here's the best part," said Julian. "Lucy made it herself!"

"You are so talented!" Avery said.

Julian grinned. Lucy's face was glowing with pride. Sure, the Blinginator had been his idea, but Lucy had taken it and created something that was 100% her.

Avery spoke up. "My cousins and I have been wanting to get matching shirts. And we love sparkles! Maybe I could pay you to make them for us?"

Lucy grinned at Julian. "Sure," she said, giving him a little punch on the arm. He had been right.

"So where are you off to?" Avery asked.

"To hang out at the park for a little while. I have soccer practice and Julian has art class this afternoon," said Lucy.

"Well, I'm going to What's the Scoop. Want to accompany me?" Avery asked.

"Yes!" Lucy shouted. "I've still got some money left on my gift card." But then her face fell. "Oh nuts, I forgot it at home." She looked at Julian.

Julian shrugged. "I don't have any money either," he said.

Avery patted her pocket. "Don't worry," she said. "It's my treat!"

Lucy and Julian exchanged glances. Maybe Avery wasn't so bad after all!

When they got to the ice-cream parlor, Avery ordered a root beer float. Julian, who loved all things chocolate, got the Death by Hot Fudge sundae. And to Lucy's great delight, there was a brand-new flavor called Jelly Doughnut. She got that, of course. A double scoop!

"Will that be cash, credit, or debit?" asked the cashier.

"Credit," said Avery, pulling out her card.

Lucy whispered to Avery, "I think you might mean debit."

The cashier scanned the card. "Yup, she's right. It's a debit card."

Avery put her hands on her hips. "Whoa, I had no idea you were such a money master!" she said.

"It's one of her superpowers," Julian said. "Along with rock climbing and burping the alphabet." Suddenly his eyes lit up. "That's it!" he cried, reaching into his backpack.

"What's it?" Lucy asked.

Julian opened his sketchbook and grinned. "I just figured out my new comic book!"

MOOLA MAN'S MONEY MATTERS
Rescue at the Register by Julian J.

DOLLARS and SenSe: SPending

Lucy almost spent all her birthday money on one blingy sweatshirt. But thanks to her best friend Julian, she ended up with a gift that keeps on giving! Not everyone is a saver like Julian. It can be very tempting to spend money as soon as you receive it. Here are some helpful hints to get more bang for your bucks!

1) Figure out if what you are planning to buy is a want or a need. If you outgrow your sneakers, that's a need. If you are buying your tenth pair, that's a want.
2) Buy things that YOU truly will enjoy, don't buy something because it is trendy or might impress your friends.
3) Try to wait until it goes on sale. It might sell out, but you could also end up getting it for a more reasonable price. (And sometimes if you put your purchase on hold, after time has passed you may realize you didn't really want it after all.)
4) Shop around! You may get a better price for the same item at another store.
5) But make sure that it's the same quality. A cheap price can sometimes mean cheap materials.

Don't miss book #2 in the Dollars to Doughnuts series!

Oops! After Julian's blender blunder, his and Lucy's cooking club looks like a horror show. Worse yet, the school's brand-new banner is ruined. Julian feels awful. He doesn't have money to replace it. With some clever budget tips and the cooking club's help, maybe Julian and Lucy can find a way to make lots of dough!

For more, visit kanepress.com